Five Passages Through Space Or Time

When harvesting furniture from the local forest, one must always make sure no one else uses it.

Sleeping on rooftops sometimes leads to unexpected adventures.

When leaving the past behind, make sure it doesn't follow you.

Discover the effects of an unreliable shipping service.

When a piece of your childhood falls, how will you bring it back?

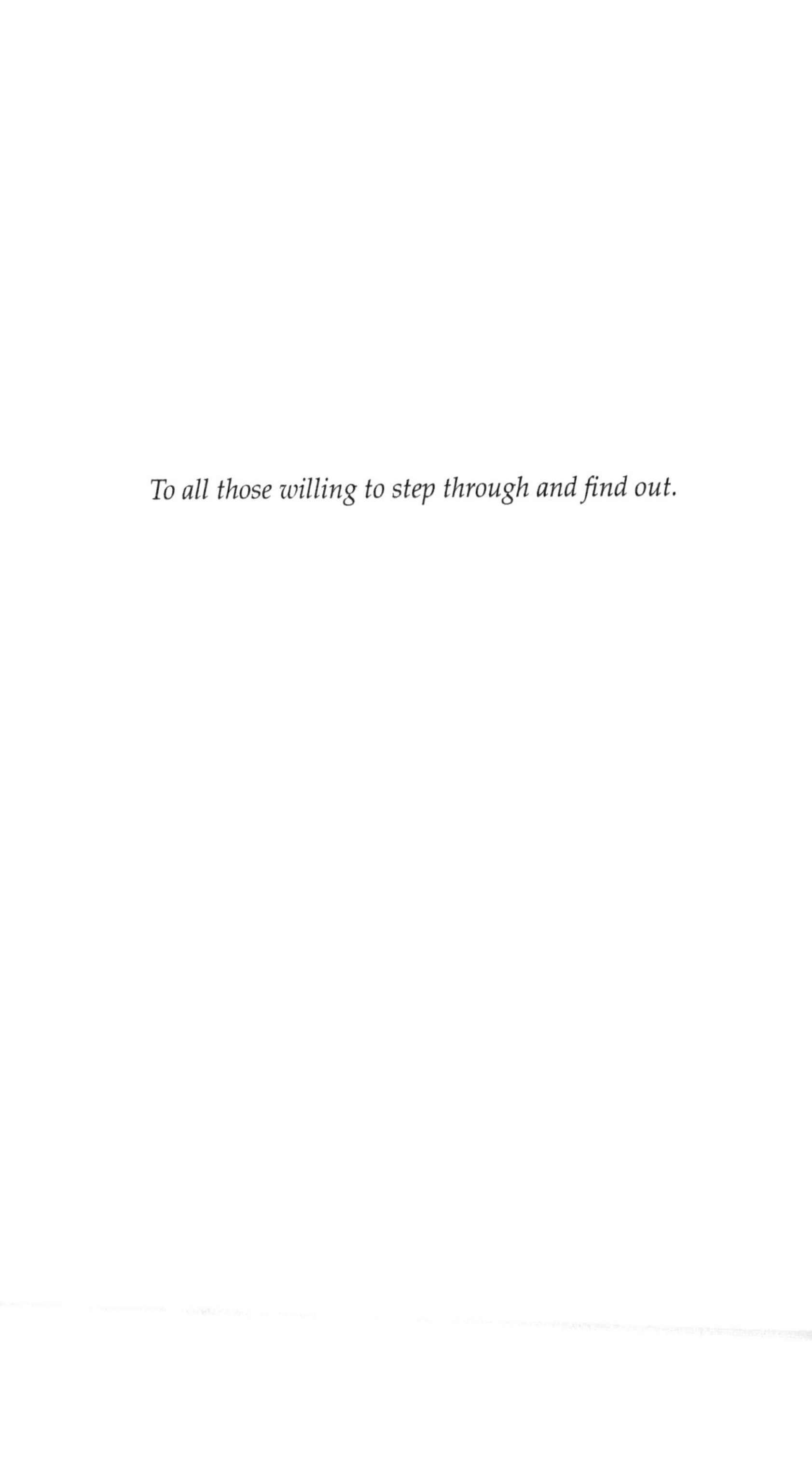

To all those willing to step through and find out.

THROUGH THE SQUIRREL TREE

TIDBITS FROM THE JASONIC STORY WELL

JASON A. ADAMS

SPIRAL PUBLISHING, LTD.

CONTENTS

INTRODUCTION

Portals. Doorways. Windows to another time and place.

Whatever you call certain openings, you know the special ones lead to somewhere different and marvelous!

Hello! And welcome to my worlds.

Who doesn't want to visit another world from time to time? I know I certainly do. That's one reason I write. I enjoy putting my flights of fancy into a more permanent record, and revisiting them later on. I call my stories the acorns collected by my Brain Squirrels, for no other reason than it tickles me.

As for the particular pile of acorns currently in your hands or on your device? I've always found stories of stepping through from one world to another fascinating. From Edgar Rice Burroughs' John Carter to the teleporting and time-traveling dragons of Anne McCaffrey's Pern, instant access to the new and strange always entertains me, as I'm sure it does yourself.

In this collection of five brand-new speculative tales

of the thinness between times, dimensions, and places, you'll discover strangeness, fear, joy, and hope. Marital compromise, pasts left behind, and intrusive futures. Delivery mix-ups, career changes, and the power of childhood memories to heal.

Fiction, by its very nature, is a portal in and of itself. Stories give us a chance to peek in on the lives of others. To suffer and triumph along with the characters. To feel their joys and sorrows. To worry for their safety, and cheer when they succeed.

We'll begin with the story of the good intentions that sometimes cause a bit of strain in a marriage, but ultimately turn out for the best.

Following that, we'll meet a lonely vagrant who unwittingly finds himself in exactly the same place, just not the same when.

Next, another story about partners who have worked hard to change their lives, and have no intention of changing them back, no matter how much is offered.

We'll meet one of those steadfast and reliable gentlemen who prefer a changeless and routine life, even if the mail goes awry.

Finally, we close with a tale of wonder, featuring a lifelong bachelor who finds new friends in the midst of a loss that shakes his spirit as much as it shakes the mountainside.

From the North Georgia mountains to Las Vegas to Atlanta to Akron to the forested slopes of the Appalachians, these tales span the United States as I've known them, or as they exist in my imagination.

So come and enter the lives of those you will meet within these pages. Join them on their journeys as they face pushy potential employers, time policemen, grumpy forest dwellers, confused collection agents, and master arborists.

One final thought. No story is truly complete until it is read. Thank you for completing mine.

Thank you for stepping through the doorway with me.

JASON A. ADAMS

Author of *Agonist* and *Mick of Malvern*

The Dangers of Cat Trees

Because Sometimes
Good Ideas Go Bad

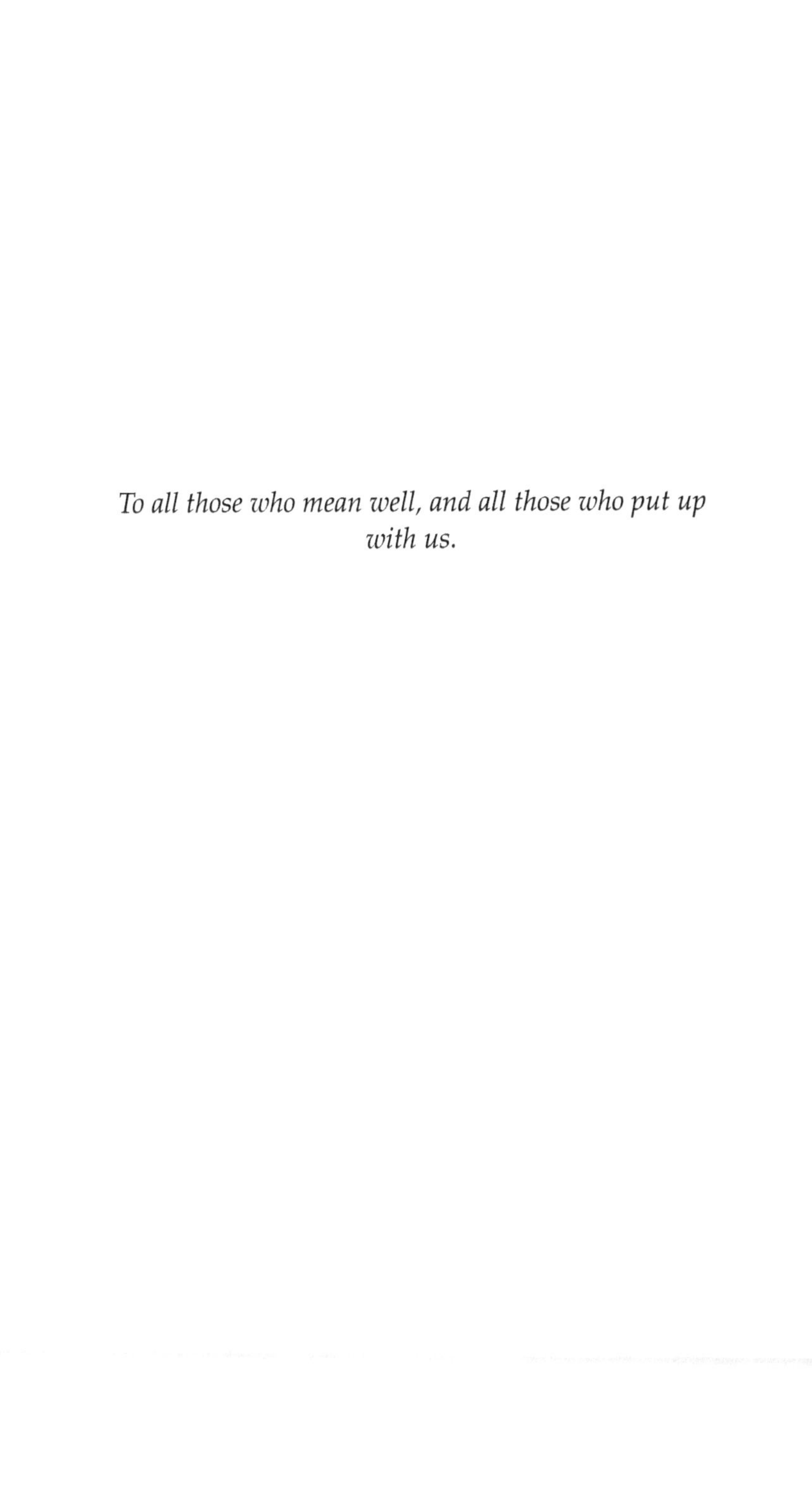

To all those who mean well, and all those who put up with us.

Chapter 1

Lord save us all from husbands with hammers.

Anne tried not to laugh out loud as she thought this, but it sure wasn't easy. Especially not when a whole corner of the already cramped living room now looked like the woods had invaded. Her overstuffed easy chair was now pushed up against the couch, instead of under the window where she had light and a breeze. And she had no idea how they'd get to half the books on the black IKEA bookshelf, now trapped behind Drew's masterpiece.

Like there wasn't enough wood in this house already. Her uncle had built this cabin in the Virginia mountains back in the Seventies, using boards inside and out that were milled from the old family home-place's logs. The hemlock walls would give you splinters if you weren't careful.

Come to think of it, he'd been a husband too.

At her feet sat Loretta, the cat they'd found wandering around an abandoned coal mine. Covered with long black hair, she looked like a bushy lump of coal. Gold eyes stared up at Anne as Loretta gave a little chirrup, obviously wondering what the hell the thing in the corner was supposed to be.

AJ, Loretta's twenty-five-pound tuxedo monster of a brother, was nowhere to be seen. He'd vamoosed early on.

Smart kitty.

Drew knelt on the floor, driving the last of the eight giant bolts he insisted were necessary to anchor the cats' new perch.

Anne had to admit it looked sturdy.

They'd decided to get the cats a bigger cat tree when a new kitten arrived, in the form of a pitiful and bedraggled ball of damp tabby. Anne had heard it mewing under one of her rose bushes a couple of weeks ago, and that was that.

She and Drew made noises about finding the poor little thing a new home, but they'd been looking for a new home for the other cats for several years now.

As kitty foster parents, they were abject failures.

Anne took Drew to the local pet store to pick a cat tree out. Drew looked at the price tags, snorted, and decided that *he*, manly man that he was, would build one himself.

Her mamma hadn't raised no dummies, but Anne kept quiet.

Several days and a dumptruck's worth of cuss words later, Drew was putting the final touches on his typically over-engineered version of classy cat quarters.

Not satisfied with the "puny straws" the real things were built of, Drew had gone out into the woods and cut down an actual tree. A red maple nearly two feet thick. The middle section with a bunch of heavy branches still sticking out.

At least she'd talked him into trimming them back before he cut a hole in the wall to bring it in.

He said he picked this tree because he liked the big knothole in the trunk. After checking for bees and owl leavings, Drew scraped out the punky black rot and smoothed the inside into a passable cat cave. The bottom sat a few inches below the opening, so the cats could get in there and hide.

Between what remained of the branches, he'd slung scraps of carpet, old burlap bags, and anything else he didn't have to spend money on.

Anne figured *she'd* be spending some money on carpet freshener to get rid of the mildewy stink.

He finally stood and presented the finished project with a wide flourish of his arms, grinning and looking as proud as an eight-year-old with his first Cub Scout birdhouse.

"Whatcha think?" he said, sucking blood from his thumb. Once he got a band-aid on it, that would make six.

Anne cleared her throat, bringing up a gob of maple-syrup-flavored sawdust. She looked at Drew's puppy-boy face and swallowed rather than spitting it out.

"Well," she said, questing for positivity. "It certainly looks like it'll last a few years."

She got closer, making a show of inspecting all the different cat perches and slings.

"I like the way you finally found a use for all that torn-up carpeting."

"Told you it would come in handy someday."

To her credit, she didn't swat him, just picked

Tibby-Tab the kitten up and put her on a piece of horrid beige shag. Tibby-Tab jumped down immediately and scooted out through the kitchen.

"Did you put it over a hole in the floor or something?" she asked.

"No, why?"

"Nothing, never mind," she said, feeling around inside the cat cave.

She could have sworn she felt a breeze coming from the big knothole. A breeze that smelled of seawater.

Nah. Just her imagination. Had to be.

Chapter 2

"AJ, NO!"

Anne snatched up an armful of evil, murderous cat as Drew flapped a towel at the bird fluttering around the living room.

Poor thing had to be scared to death. Of course, Anne was pretty spooked herself.

How the hell had a *bird* gotten in?

"Come on," Drew crooned in a singsong. "C'mere, you little shit."

The bird, its black-and-white stripes flashing as it did an aerial scuttle along the crown molding, didn't look local. Anne wasn't much of a birder herself, but she'd never seen one with stripes like that. Or with a beak the color of a half-ripe blueberry.

Probably some pet that got loose, then found its way into their living room.

"Hah! Gotcha, you dirty—shit!"

Drew almost got the towel over the interloper, but not before it flew straight into the kitty cave in his majestic eyesore of a cat tree.

He started to reach inside, and Anne grabbed his arm.

"Maybe you should put some gloves on, honey," she said. And managed not to pinch the bejeezus out her handyman's skin.

"Hm. Good point."

Drew fetched his fireplace gloves while Anne held the towel over the knothole, a makeshift and hopefully bird-proof cell door. She caught that whiff of salt and seaweed again. She'd have to spray some bleach in there, kill whatever mildew or mold made it smell like that.

"Careful," she said, easing the towel away as Drew reached into the hole in the trunk.

He reached upward. Said something his mamma would swat him for. Groped around.

Anne stood by, towel at the ready.

"You got it?"

"No," he said, now feeling along the bottom. "I don't think it's in here."

"Has to be," she said. "Where else *would* it be?"

"Must've snuck out while I was getting my gloves. C'mon, let's go track it down before it poops on something."

Anne was pretty sure she'd have noticed a pigeon-sized intruder sneaking past her towel, but she kept her mouth shut.

They split up, checked all the windows and doors, upstairs and down.

No holes in the screens. No errant breezes to tell of any new gaps in wall, ceiling, or floor.

"Okay," Anne said, giving up on bird hunting for the day. "Let's lock the cats in the bedroom and open the doors and windows. Maybe it'll find its way back out."

Chapter 3

THERE *HAD* to be a hole somewhere.

Over the last three days, Anne and Drew had chased birds, faced down a squirrel with shaggy red hair like some rodent Viking, and even caught a glimpse of something that might have been a racoon, a badger, or a garbage disposal with legs.

Lots of teeth, anyhow.

But no matter what genius tactics or how many towels and bedsheets they used, the invaders always slipped the net.

The cats were no help.

Loretta went as far as to chitter at the cat tree where the birds sometimes settled. AJ had decided that under the bed was far preferable to the Wild Kingdom in the rest of the house.

Tibby-Tab thought the various critters were playmates, and kept busy chasing them around, getting under Anne's feet at the worst possible times.

Anne was starting to wonder about that stupid tree in the living room.

Of course there was no way wildlife could come and go through that knothole.

But Loretta kept making her *there's a bird in the yard* noises.

And AJ the Billy-Bobcat wouldn't go near it.

And Tibby-Tab *really* wanted to check it out, but her tiny claws couldn't quite make the climb.

And then there was that seaside odor.

Anne didn't smell it all the time. But way too often.

What exactly did one do when some sort of magical interdimensional gateway seemed to be embedded in one's cat tree?

Drew was still convinced something had chewed a hole through the siding, possibly up in the ceiling crawlspace.

She could hear him thumping around up there, after squeezing himself through the two-by-two access hole in the closet ceiling.

She was pretty sure he wouldn't find anything.

Flashlight in fireplace-gloved hand, Anne left Drew to his handy-manning and went to the knothole in that stupid maple tree in her friggin' living room.

The smell was stronger today.

Anne flicked on the flashlight and looked inside the hole.

And promptly dropped the flashlight.

The inside of the knothole was already brightly lit. By warm, yellow light.

Like sunlight.

From high up inside the trunk, Anne thought she heard seagulls crying.

That was crazy. Right?

She barely choked back a scream as something rubbed against her ankle.

"Dammit, Tibby-Tab. Now is *not* the time to pester mamma!"

Scooting the obnoxious kitten with her toe, Anne closed her eyes, counted to three, and looked back into the knothole, hoping to see nothing but pitch-darkness and smell nothing but syrup and damp wood.

Somehow she wasn't surprised to see someone staring right back at her.

Chapter 4

ANNE MAGICALLY TRANSPORTED BACKWARD a couple of feet. If she'd been sitting, she'd have done a gold-medal butt scoot.

A strange little man stood in the knothole, scowling at her from between gigantic white eyebrows and a beard Santa would have sold his sleigh for.

"Who the hell built a bleedin' house around my blinkin' transport tree?"

Anne clapped her hands over her ears. For a guy not much taller than her kneecap, he sounded like a pro wrestler in full monologue.

She tried to answer, felt her jaw flapping around without much success. So she swallowed and tried again.

"Um, I don't mean to be rude, but did you come from inside the tree?"

His beady old eyes rolled magnificently.

"Who the bloody bollocks comes from inside a tree? D'you think I'm some sort of bloomin' acorn?"

"But...but the knothole doesn't—"

"Tisn't a knothole, ye great gobshite. 'Tis the Vacation Gate. Although why the Gatekeepers thought I'd want to vacation in yon horrid woodpile is a mystery for the ages."

Pretty rude for a houseguest.

"Vacation gate?" There. That was enough words for now.

"Aye, did I stutter? The doorway to beach and bliss. Do your ilk not venture afar for rest and relaxation and se...fun?"

She nodded. Tibby-Tab purred around her ankles. Loretta chittered. AJ stayed under the bed.

Taking a closer look, Anne noticed the baggy shorts and palm-tree-covered shirt the little guy wore. Give him a miniature fanny-pack, and he'd look like a poster boy for Old Farts Travel.

"I'm sorry," she said. "We didn't know this was your tree. My husband cut it down to make a roost for our cats."

"Humph. Explains a bit." He stuck his head out far enough to take in the bits of fabric serving as cat slings, the bookshelf, her chair, and various other non-forest surroundings.

"That your man kicking up ruckus above?"

Anne nodded.

"Well, he needs to hie his shaker down here and help me get my tree back where it belongs."

The little man snapped his fingers, the sound like a gunshot.

Drew suddenly appeared, covered with cobwebs and bits of pink insulation.

"What the—"

She couldn't blame him for being a little startled. She certainly wasn't *un*-startled.

"Drew, honey, I'd like you to meet…er…"

"Conaill, at your service," said the pipsqueak in the knothole, bowing until his beard hung out the opening.

"Uh, there's a miniature man in our cat tree."

Give Drew a trophy for his steel-trap mind.

"Man?? I'll give ye man, you great—"

The little guy, Conaill, was fixing to snap those fingers again, and that couldn't be good.

"Ix-nay on the an-may, Drew."

Again with the prize-winning eyeroll.

"Such a clever and diabolical code. Just help me get my tree back where it belongs, and I won't be forced to clap you in sandpaper knickers for the rest of your life."

Chapter 5

With a few finger snaps, it didn't take long for the tree/gate/eyesore to vacate Anne's living room, for which she was profoundly grateful.

Conaill the whatever-he-was carried the top, leaving the much heavier base to Drew. Considering the way the miniature not-man held his end with one hand, Anne was pretty sure he was giving himself far more help than poor sweaty Drew got.

Once the tree was standing more-or-less straight on its stump, Conaill gave another artillery-shell finger snap, sealing trunk and stump together. Branches regrew, and within a couple of minutes, the maple tree stood tall and proud as ever, covered with thick green foliage that nearly hid the knothole in the trunk.

"I want to apologize again for disturbing your Vacation Gate," Anne said. "I know how hard it can be to get away from work."

"You know not the half of it, dearie," Conaill said. "But, I see neither harm nor foul now that all's set to rights."

Drew leaned against the trunk, still sweating and rubbing his shoulders.

"Guess I'll have to find another tree," he grumbled. "Maybe an oak or hickory this—"

A loud report echoed from the hills all around. Anne covered her ears, saw Conaill blowing smoke from his fingers.

Drew had gone still as a statue.

"What did you do to Drew?" she said. "Did you hurt him? I'll—"

"Calm yourself, girlie," Conaill said. "I'm no scholar of humans, but I have been married for over six hundred years, and I recognize good intentions and the annoyance they can bring."

Drew blinked sleepily, looked around at the trees before finally noticing Anne.

"You can thank me some other time," Conaill said as he disappeared back into the magical knothole.

Anne grabbed Drew's chin. Checked his eyes.

"Are you okay, honey?"

"Huh?" Drew still looked a little out of it, but seemed to be coming around. "Yeah. I'm fine. Just thinking."

He held her hand and started back toward the house.

"You know, using a real tree seems like a lot of trouble. Probably be easier to just buy that Super Cat Deluxe Hotel from the pet store. That okay with you?"

"Thank you, Conaill," Anne whispered.

Out loud, she said, "Sure, Drew. Whatever you think best."

They went back home to change before heading to town for a proper cat tree.

Maybe she would hide Drew's hammers once they got home.

Just to stay on the safe side.

JASON A. ADAMS

Author of *GS-304* and *Sunlit Dispositions*

Temporal Fallout

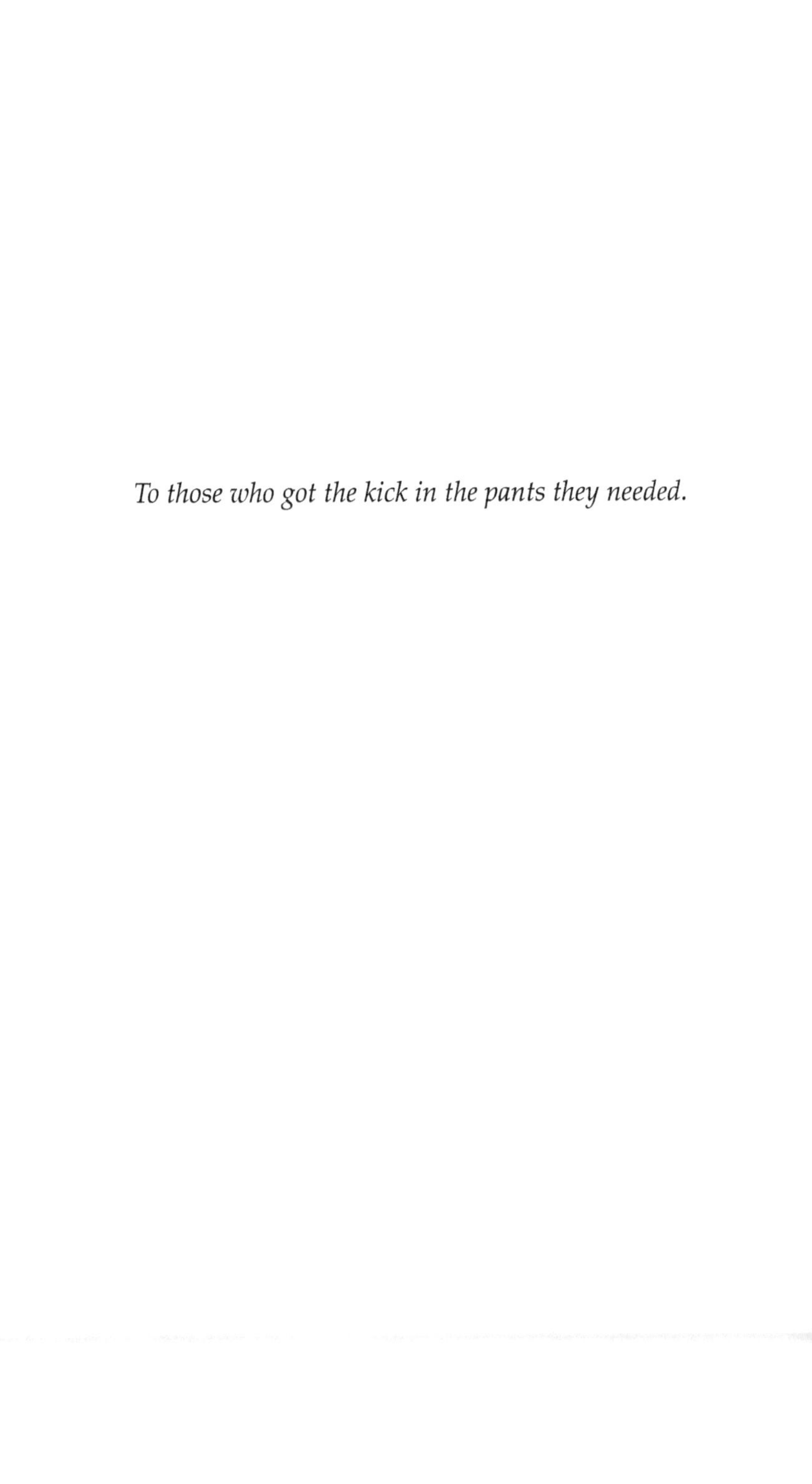

To those who got the kick in the pants they needed.

Chapter 1

Nothing like a rooftop hideaway. Especially one under the stars in Las Vegas.

Livin' large, livin' rich. Not bad for a defrocked lawyer with no home, no practice, and no money.

Sylvester Dotson, ex-Esq., jerked out of his half-sleep wanderings when something hit his leg.

He peeled his crusty eyelids apart, squinting against eye-stabbing sunlight as the owner of the mirror-polished black shoes muttered a "sorry, mac" and hurried on past.

Those black shoes and pin-striped slacks weren't the only legs, though. All around him, excited voices yammered back and forth as their bodies milled by, heading toward the roof's edge.

And the roof was wrong, too. Where were all the bus-sized chilling towers?

Sylvester had snuck onto the Golden Nugget's roof last night, creeping out one of the service exits, the one with the busted camera. He liked snoozing up here when the weather was cool, leaned up against the roof's raised edge, up above the Freemont Street Experience's big canopy. Hidden from all the suckers shelling out too much cash for worthless tourist crap down below. No one bothered him, no cops, no people. And it was up above all the racket of the Fremont Street Hellhole.

Usually, anyway.

Today, the honking and rumble of traffic sounded louder than normal. And coming from the wrong direction.

The roof swarmed with people. People dressed awful weird, too.

The guys all wore blue or black suits and Bogart-looking hats. Huge pads puffed their shoulders out, giving them the look of faux linebackers. The women all had dresses on, so tight around the butt and thighs he didn't see how they could walk.

And high heels. And gloves.

No shorts, no loud cabana wear, no t-shirts with stupid touristy crap on them.

Weird.

All of them had one thing in common. They were all puffing away like steam trains on cancer sticks. A few had pipes or cigars, but all of them were lit up. Even the chicks.

Sylvester couldn't help but notice he didn't see The Plaza's ugly white tower through the toxic haze. Up on top of the Nugget, he should be looking straight across to just below the Plaza's penthouses.

Now it wasn't there.

He eased up and looked over the ledge. Instead of the curved FSE roof with all the girders and wiring for the LED show, he could see down all of fifteen feet into a mess of cars jamming up Fremont Street. Cars belching blue smoke and blatting their horns.

Old cars. Even a couple of Studebakers.

The stink of all that exhaust clawed up his nose and down his throat, coating the back of his tongue. He ducked back down behind the low wall, rubbing his watery eyes.

What the hell was going on? Another movie, maybe? But how the hell did they get rid of the gigantic canopy?

And why was *his* roof all wrong?

Then he noticed the top of The Fremont's big corner sign sticking up across the way. Once upon a time, that had been the tallest building in the state. The only thing he saw that came close to topping it was Vegas Vic.

The giant neon cowboy waved his arms right beside a row of metal letters full of lightbulbs. Vic winked and gave out a booming "HOWDY, PARDNER!!"

The Pioneer Club. That place went away when Sylvester was just a kid.

And Vic hadn't spoken since the Sixties, so far as he knew.

Around Vic, mile high signs marked The Boulder Club, the Lucky Strike, Hotel Apache, and a bunch of other now-defunct hotels and casinos. The lights in their signs were on, even in the daytime, and looked to be restored to the original tiny bulbs instead of the LED rigs most places had now.

Must've brought all the signs in from the neon graveyard for the movie, right?

Maybe?

But that didn't explain why he was looking *up* at

those signs, instead of down from one of the Nugget's tall hotel towers.

Maybe he'd finally gone nutso. The lady at the clinic told him all the cheap liquor might eventually do his brain a mischief or two.

More and more oddball people rushed past him, heading toward the northwest corner of the roof. Some wore sparkly, rhinestone-studded cateye sunglasses. Some carried boxy square things that looked like old-time Kodaks on straps around their necks.

A flash of diamond-bright light appeared in the distance and flushed the sun away. Everyone *oohed* and pointed.

Sylvester hunkered, pulling his knees up to his chin.

The light dimmed a little, and a minute later the whole building shook like a big one had just hit the San Andreas.

Above the heads of the crowd, he saw a glowing ball of hell rising on top of a narrow column of smoke.

Was that a goddamn *mushroom cloud??*

He didn't hear any of the air raid sirens like on TV. No one panicked or seemed the least bit upset.

Half of them clapped and cheered. The other half looked down into their boxy contraptions and snapped photos.

Overhead, a pair of silvery, needle-shaped jet fighter planes screeched by.

The heat. He must've slept too late, and gotten his noggin baked.

Except it felt like maybe seventy degrees right now. And the sign at the Four Queens had showed seventy-six last night.

Maybe he needed water. He was awful thirsty. Time

to head down and find a water fountain without any casino goons watching.

At least no one in the crowd was looking his way. He got up, slow and careful, and headed back to the service hatch.

Which wasn't where it had been the night before. Shit!

What in the ever-lovin' hell was going on around here?

"Hey, over here," someone said.

Sylvester looked to his left, saw a different stairwell hutch. In the doorway stood a dude in the same dark blue gangster suit and hat as the rest of the local menfolk. His horsey face was pale as a skull, and he wore heavy black horn-rim glasses with lenses so thick they turned his hazel eyes into dinner plates.

Sylvester thought the guy had a spinal problem until he noticed it was because the dude had to stoop to keep his head from bumping the top of the doorway. UNLV must've lusted after him for the bucket-ball team.

"Move it, laughing boy. Hup-hup!" He snapped his fingers at Sylvester.

Asshole. But at least he seemed to have a clue. Sylvester wasn't sure what kind of clue, but at this point he'd take what he could get.

He followed the beanpole down the stairs. All the way down.

Two whole flights.

"What's going on?" Sylvester asked El Oddball. "Did I go crazy or something? Who are you, anyway? And why should I go with you?"

At the foot of the stairs, the guy stopped. Inside, where he could stand up straight, he looked like a green bean had been stretched out. Close to seven feet, probably. And about as big around as a pencil.

He looked directly at Sylvester—well, directly down at him—and Sylvester saw rows of backward writing filling the lenses of the hornrims. Like tiny little computer screens.

"I am Avenir Garamond," he said, going rigid as a frozen girder. "Watch Sergeant First Class, Global Temporal Containment Force, Three-Fifty-Sixth Intercept Squadron. And you are Sylvester Leonard Dotson, one-time attorney and now full-time vagrant."

Yep, Sylvester had cracked his pot. Definitely. Or else Avewhatsis had.

"Uh-huh. Sure, buddy. Thanks for the trip down the stairs, but I think I'll just mosey on along."

Sylvester reached for the door handle, forgetting all the bizarro stuff outside. His first priority was to get away from this wacko.

Whose ridiculously long arm had just whipped out, catching Sylvester right below the neck.

"I'm afraid I can't let you do that. The interrupts to the integrity of Terra Timeline 26X are already straining the future."

Sylvester blinked. That was about all he could manage. Sure, he'd been an alky bum for a couple of years, but he'd been pretty sharp in law school and did a lot of reading when he could.

Helped him appreciate just how little of the Sarge's speech he really understood.

"What the hell are you talking about?"

Sarge opened the door, took Sylvester's left arm in a grip surprisingly strong for such a skinny guy, and hustled him out onto the street, then around the corner and toward a boarded-up place that might have been a bar, but now had paper posters advertising the new Brown Stetson steakhouse, opening soon.

Sarge pulled a small box with a couple of rods sticking out, pointed it at the door and pressed something. A tiny buzz came from both box and door, and Sarge pushed it open and dragged him through into…

Into a brightly lit space lined with gleaming white tables or desks or something. From several places along the long workspace, low black cubes projected screens onto matte-gray walls, displaying graphs, spiky jittering lines like EKGs, and pictures.

Including several versions of Sylvester himself.

In one, he was a young professional, in his own black suit and blood-colored necktie, proudly holding his sheepskin and shaking hands with Mr. Morton of Ellis, Morton, & Stanley, the firm he'd joined straight out of school, and washed out of three short years later.

He'd learned more about Jack Daniels than he had about litigation theory at UNLV's Boyd School of Law, and it caught up with him after one too many slurred closing statements.

Another showed him sleeping in a doorway, wrapped in the threadbare army surplus blanket he'd used until a bigger and meaner street denizen relieved him of it one night, along with his backpack and a mostly intact pair of Skechers.

The third showed him running down this archaic version of Fremont, while three goons in pinstriped suits pointed guns at his back.

"We need to correct your situation, Mr. Dotson," Sarge said. "Or at least get you in some clothes more suitable to the current temporal position. If you die in what you're wearing, anachronistic entanglements will upset at least three different timelines and lead to… well, to problems down the road."

"Die?? What do you mean, die?" And yesterday had been such a good day. He'd gotten most of a Happy Meal from a mother with a bitchy tween. Twenty bucks, mostly paper, from the marks coming off the Experience. He'd even taken a quick bath when a groundskeeper offered him a hose-down.

Sarge sighed. Flicked his fingers toward one of the display cube things. Brought up a newspaper clipping from the *Las Vegas Sun* dated February 23, 1955.

The headline read *MYSTERY MAN MURDERED IN BROAD DAYLIGHT.*

Below the headline was a photo of his own face, only looking a lot more dead than he usually did.

Yesterday evening, three gangsters presumably from the Frazetta mob shot and killed a man on Fremont Street in cold blood. The victim, who has not yet been identified, has baffled both police officers and members of the Clark County Sheriff's Department.

"I've never seen clothes like these," said Officer Thaddeus Barton of the LVPD. "The shoes, the slacks. And the dough he had? It's gotta be fake. The dates—"

--Story continues on A8

"You see the problem, don't you?" Sarge said. "Soon after you die, rumors begin of aliens. Soviet infiltration. Secret government experiments. The John Birch Society gains more traction, and things really go off the beam."

Sylvester could only stare at the picture of his dead face.

"This is some sort of scam, right?" He hated the whine in his voice, but felt worse whining on the move. "I mean, why would anyone come after me?"

"Because, Mr. Dotson, you are out of place. Out of time. Out of sync with the people around you. People sense that, and it makes them a bit uncomfortable. As you are currently uncomfortable, unless I am very much mistaken."

Mistaken? Shit. Uncomfortable didn't really touch it at all.

"But what can I do about it? How do I go back? I don't even have any idea how I got here."

"That's the simple part," Sarge said, twiddling his fingers and bringing up an image of another nuke cloud. "The above-ground thermonuclear detonations at the nearby facility operated by this century's military. The addition of Lithium-7 to the cores of then-now-current devices results in stresses along the temporal continuum, with the occasional inconvenient displacement of organic material. Like yourself. My team's remit is to correct such displacements, thus dissolving unstable timelines and keeping divergent futures down to a sustainable level."

Sylvester nodded. Safest approach.

"Another detonation will be occurring in approximately one hundred and fifty-three hours. My colleagues will adjust the temporal threads, and we should be able to return you to your then-current continuum location with an accuracy of plus or minus two percent. Clear?"

Sylvester nodded again. Did some quick math in his head.

"A whole week? What the hell am I supposed to do for a week? Besides not getting shot."

A smile cracked open Sarge's face. Not an especially comforting smile, but who knew how to read a seven-foot-tall, first-class temporal intercept guy's expression?

"For now, Mr. Dotson, I'd like you to watch something with me."

Another flap of those long fingers, and the nearest projector cube doohickey flashed up a series of colored bands.

As Sylvester watched, the bands began to writhe like snakes. Wove back and forth through and across each other.

Pretty. And relaxing.

He could watch this all day.

All—

Chapter 2

"COME, Mr. Dotson. Time to go. Hup-hup!"

Sylvester jerked.

"Huh? What? Time to go where?"

Shit, he felt stiff. And his mouth tasted some dead frog's ass.

"Time to return you to your perch on the roof nearby. The *Moth* detonation is in less than half an hour."

"Half an hour? I thought you said I had to wait a week."

That not-quite-cheerful smile was back. "Oh, being a member of the GTCF, I have a few specialized tools at my disposal. Including a way to keep you in a state of hypno-stasis for the necessary time. Come now, we need to get you back to your proper coordinates. Hup-hup!"

Sylvester followed Sarge back out to the street. He was pretty sure things would make sense after whatever was in his system wore off or he puked it out.

The street was still full of classic cars. The women

still wore skirts that only let their legs work from the knee down. Everyone still sucked lungfuls of cigarette smoke.

He didn't see the goons from the one picture, so that was good.

Back to the Nugget's service door. Back up the two flights of stairs to the way-too-low rooftop.

A crowd already waited at the edge of the roof, eyeballs and camera lenses pointed off to the northwest.

"Sit, Mr. Dotson. Try to get in as close to the same position as you can."

Seemed like someone from the gawk-squad would notice a giant string bean in a suit, but no one paid Sarge or him any mind at all.

"Quickly, now. Displacement can occur anywhere from five to ten—"

Sylvester's ears popped like he was on the express elevator and his stomach flopped like a fish freshly yanked onto dry land.

The traffic noise vanished, except for a low rumble way off in the distance.

And Sarge was gone. Along with the crowd of nuke tourists.

All around him towered the massive cubes of modern Las Vegas air chilling equipment.

He couldn't see any of the postcard signage anywhere. He *could* see straight across to the penthouse rooms at the Plaza, where a couple were currently giving the city a Penthouse view, getting-lucky style.

Bless them and happy romping!

Beside his leg, Sylvester saw the neck of a bottle peeking out from a brown paper bag. He kicked bottle and bag as hard as he could, sending them skittering across the roof.

Time to find Father Dolan. Time to take him up on his offer of help finding a rehab.

But not to go to confession. Sylvester thought maybe he'd keep this particular dream or whatever to himself.

At least until he got past the bar exams again. After that, who knew?

Maybe he'd specialize in temporal law someday.

Whistling a few bars of *They're Coming To Take Me Away*, Sylvester headed for the roof's access door, and toward whatever came next.

JASON A. ADAMS

Author of *GS-304* and *Sunlit Dispositions*

Career Choices

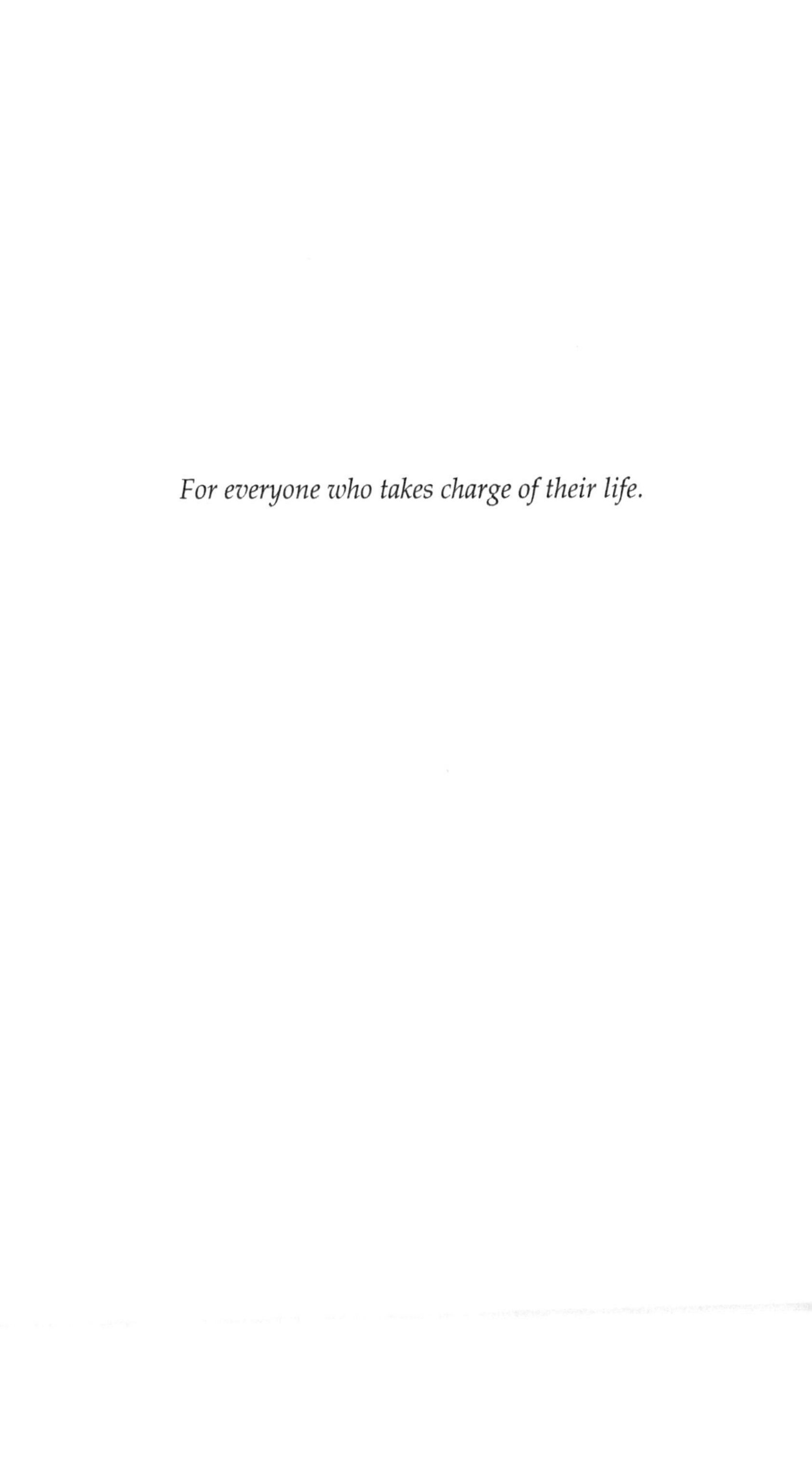

For everyone who takes charge of their life.

Chapter 1

Never involve accountants in equipment purchases.

Blake Thompson stared at the unblinking lights on the main email server. No cooling fans whirred happily. No slightly eye-stinging smell of hot electronics. No overheated air filling the space around the rack, in spite of air conditioning that barely made a dent in Atlanta's miserable muggy summer atmosphere.

Probably the flippin' power socket. Not the first time, either.

He shouldn't be surprised. Wickman and Barnard Accounting wasn't his most spendy client.

Take the server room, for instance. Instead of systems any third grader could recognize, the two racks stuffed into what had probably been a supply closet judging from the stench of ghosts of cleansers past bore servers with names like Dale Computing Systems, IMB Server Technology, and—his favorite—Pear.

He squeezed behind the rack as best he could, trying not to sneeze from the stink of ancient floor treatment that tried to coat his sinuses and tongue, (Mr. Not Dirty, no doubt) and checked the plug. Sure enough, the heavy cable jiggled loosely in the socket on the back of the dead machine.

C13 universal power cables were only as old as, you know, servers. How the heck could a manufacturer mess up the socket so badly?

Oh, well. Make do, improvise.

Taking a roll of good ol' black electrical tape from his pocket, Blake pulled the plug from the back of the server and proceeded to wrap it in several layers. Not a permanent solution, but should keep the server up and running for a few months until the tape broke down.

Before reinserting the mummified plug, Blake took a tube from his other pocket, squeezed a drop of clear liquid on his fingertip, and smeared the slippery goo over the tape.

Slik-Glide was fantastic stuff. Besides its original use as a lubricant for activities of the boudoir variety, the silicone-based gel would keep the tape on the plug from melting against the socket's walls.

He never went anywhere without a tube. Hadn't since he'd first run across it while working his way through his certification courses a decade ago.

Better than WD-30, and easier to carry around. Plus, it didn't cause rashes.

Blake wormed his way out of the claustrophobic space behind the rack, and hit the Pear's power button. Grinned when all the proper lights went blinky-blink and the internal hard drives hummed to life.

A few minutes to make sure the OS loaded properly and the email services started, and he could collect his $250 emergency call fee and get the hell out of here.

Chapter 2

Two hours and a promise to wipe every drive in the place if Wickman and Barnard didn't pay in full on the spot later, Blake finally got back to the office.

Parker-Thompson CompuTech didn't look like much, just a couple of beige rooms in a generic Atlanta office park where you had to leave breadcrumbs to find your particular glass door.

They had a reception desk out front, and a workbench lined with power supplies and board testers in back. He and his partner didn't keep many repair parts in stock, since computer equipment could be outdated by the time an order arrived.

Still, there was the requisite box of cables of all descriptions. Keyboards and mice, wired and wireless (including a hoary old PS2 keyboard that would outlive the Rocky Mountains). Plus assorted laptop and desktop carcasses in various stages of cannibalization.

The mouth-watering aroma of garlic, chipotle, and popcorn hit him as soon as he opened the door, letting him know his partner was in the shop and working the break room hotplate like the magician she was.

"That you, sweetie?" she called from her altar of yumminess, and he answered her summons. And the summons of food.

"Yeah, I'm back. Some of that popcorn for me, sugarplum?"

He dropped his bag on the workbench and went through to the tiny break room, kicking a random VGA cable out of the way. He really needed to organize his obsolete equipment piles one of these days.

Chelle Parker, his partner both on the job and off, stood at the long laminate countertop, dressed in her new professional uniform. Faded jeans and a snug but not tight black polo shirt. Her ponytail flipped crazily as she shook a huge, foil-covered metal salad bowl for all she was worth. The rapid machine-gunning of popcorn on the pop filled the air, along with the wonderful scent of her special seasoning blend.

Ambrosia.

Blake waited for the popping to subside and for Chelle to set the blazing hot bowl of goodness aside before wrapping her in a bear hug and kissing her cheek.

He also proudly displayed the check from the accounting firm, holding it over his head in both hands like a pro wrestler with a brand-new gold-plated belt.

Chelle clapped her hands and grabbed for the check, swatting his belly when he lifted it higher, out of her reach.

"You actually got those skinflints to *pay* you? Today? In full, even?" She planted a big, wet smooch on him. "You, Master Thompson, are truly a wizard!"

He shrugged his best ain't-no-thing shrug.

"Yeah, well. Just takes a little diplomacy and tact. You should try it sometime, m'dear."

"Uh-huh. What threat did you use?" She peeled the foil off the popcorn bowl and drizzled more of her own wizardry over the steaming kernels.

"Just a rare-earth magnet hidden somewhere inside the file server chassis. Once I explained—in small, one-syllable words—exactly what that would do to all their data, old man Barnard practically ruptured himself paying up."

Chelle laughed while Blake helped himself to a handful of spicy kernels, sucking air to keep his taste-buds intact. Popcorn really should only be eaten at a temperature slightly cooler than the sun.

He carried the bowl to the workbench in the other room, while Chelle got a couple of hourglass bottles from the mini-fridge. The Mexican version cost half again as much as American, but glass and sugar made all the difference in flavor. And Blake was an old-fash-ioned kinda guy.

They munched corn and drank bubbly Atlanta-bred cola, competing on the best and smelliest belch.

No one walking in on this little slice of family-busi-ness bliss would ever recognize Jack Hammer and Summer Peakes, once the hottest pair on brown-paper wrapped videotape.

The acting gig—and acting is exactly what it was, no one feels honestly frisky with chafed nether regions and a director telling them to speed it up, two minutes to climax—had been fun for a while. And had paid their way through school and the initial setup of the tech support and consulting business.

But trying to live a normal life wasn't easy for a guy

built like Schwarzenegger in the early years. Or for a gal with a triple-F rack, artificial or not.

Plus, it had always been awkward when they got recognized by bank execs in thousand-dollar suits, car salesmen, checkout clerks, and even the occasional soccer mom or SUV warrior.

IT work was less prone to uncomfortable conversations, and a heck of a lot easier.

All it took to go incognito had been shaving the dead lemur off his upper lip and letting his body hair grow back. Chelle had reduced her Peakes to more sensible hills and let her natural auburn replace the platinum upstairs.

Wearing clothes didn't hurt, of course.

When the bowl was empty and the bottles set in the blue recycling tub, Chelle stood and stretched.

"Oh, I forgot to tell you," she said. "We have a potential new client."

New clients were good. Usually. Unless it was another accounting firm.

"What's up, sugarplum?"

She wiped her fingers on her jeans and picked up a pocket-sized spiral notebook from the bench. He loved how she worked in a high-tech business but still stuck to paper for notes. She flipped through the miniature pages for a sec, then handed him the notebook.

"Lamppost Entertainment Group," she said, tapping the page. "Mr. Dunkel would like to see us both at ten in the morning to discuss their needs. And our fee, naturally."

"Naturally," he agreed. "Both of us? Is he wanting a full system redesign or something?"

She shook her head. "Don't think so, but he was pretty vague about things. Let's just hie our little tushies over there tomorrow morning and extort…I mean, *negotiate* a good return for our services."

"Sounds like a plan, sugarplum. And for now, let's hie our tushies back to the house. I'm ready for something more filling than popcorn, most divine though yours is."

She smiled in that innocent way of hers that always made him suspicious.

"I do believe a certain sweetie just volunteered to make his most divine crab rangoons and sesame chicken for his business associate."

"Only if you let *me* pick the dessert."

"You're on," she said with a giggle. "Pervert."

Chapter 3

THE NEXT MORNING, Chelle pulled their work van into an empty spot in front of a low, square cinderblock of a white cinderblock building. And Blake thought their office park was bland? This place had all the charm and color of an over-boiled egg.

At least the sign was cool. An antique iron gas lamp, gas flame flickering away, held a groovy wooden signboard. A hand holding a curvy placard reading *Lampost Entertainment Group, Ltd.,* the index finger pointing toward yet another glass door. Covered in smoky mirrored film, so that was a little different, at least.

Blake tried the door. Locked. He checked his watch, saw that they were five minutes early, but still.

He raised a fist to knock, but Chelle reached past him and calmly pressed a button below a much smaller sign that said *Press button for entry.*

"Smartass," he said. Quietly, though. A shadowy figure on the other side of the mirrored door was heading their way.

The door opened, revealing a scarecrow in a char-coal three-piece business suit. Double-breasted, even. Sharp. Skinny as a rail, their greeter had to be six-four in stocking feet. Jet black hair slicked back over a face he could only describe as pointy. A heavy Roman nose swooped down to a thin-lipped mouth which stretched open in a welcoming smile that put Blake in mind of a cat finding its way to The Home for Paralyzed Birds and Rodents.

"Mr. Thompson and Ms. Parker, I presume?" the greeter said in a voice deep and resonant as a good cello. Lightly accented, but not enough for Blake to place the origin. "Thank you indeed for your punctuality. *Do* come in."

"Thank you, sir," Chelle said, all diplomacy and tact. "You'd be Mr. Dunkel, right?"

"Absolutely correct, young lady. Allow me to show you to our networking room."

The only sign Chelle had heard the *young lady* remark was a slight stiffening of the spine and the sound of a bill going up at least fifteen percent.

They followed Dunkel down a long hallway, passing a few office doors with dusty knobs. Must be a one-man shop, but that suit promised an ability to pay. Willingness could be obtained by fair means or foul, if necessary.

Dunkel stopped at the last door on the right. He twisted the bright brass doorknob and opened the door with a deep bow and flourish.

"And here we are! My pride and joy."

Blake and Chelle stared at what lay inside. Blake was pretty sure his mouth was hanging open, but he didn't mind.

Inside the room, a server rack formed from intricately worked wrought iron sprouted metal leaves and vines that curled from floor to ceiling before circling out to form a shiny black ring at least eight feet across.

Within the rack nestled a…computer? Contraption?

Three shelves of glowing vacuum tubes connected with high grade fiber-optic cable. An exposed array full of gently humming solid-state drives. A thumb-thick cable of uninsulated twisted copper wire that snaked from a dull, lead-colored box at the base to a heavy reddish bronze socket on the side of the massive iron ring.

The smell of hot glass competed with ozone and…something.

"It's, um, certainly a unique setup," Blake said. Chelle wasn't the only one who could be charming. "What, uh, does it do, exactly? And what do you need us to do to it?"

Dunkel laughed. "Oh, no. You've misunderstood the situation. I didn't ask you here to repair equipment you couldn't possibly understand. No, I need you and your delightful consort for an entirely different reason, Mr. Thompson. Or should I say Mr. Hammer?"

Blake felt like he'd been slapped upside the head with a rotting fish.

"Who's Mr. Hammer?" Chelle asked, keeping herself steady much better than he was.

"Come now, Ms. Peakes. I assure you I know all about your previous work. And I am a fan. Yes, indeed. But not nearly so much as are my clients. Clients who are more than prepared to make us all three obscenely —if you'll excuse the term—wealthy."

"Okay, that's enough," Blake said. "Thanks for your time, Dunkel, but we're IT consultants and tech support. And that's it. So if you don't mind, we'll—"

"Allow me to show you something," Dunkel said, reaching out and pulling an honest-to-god blade switch straight out of a mad scientist's lab.

The humming increased, and Blake's hair started to rise as the giant iron hoop began to fill with swirling rainbow-colored mist.

"What the hell?" Chelle whispered, as the mist faded to reveal what looked like a town square surrounded by squat adobe structures.

A town square *way* too big to fit inside a modest Atlanta office space.

"Shall we?" Dunkel said, clutching both Blake and Chelle by the arm before stepping through the ring.

And dragging the two of them along with him.

Chapter 4

A split skin-tingling second later, Blake's skin erupted in goosebumps.

Adobe buildings or not, the dusty town square had to be thirty degrees cooler than the city he should by all rights be standing in.

And where exactly had his clothes gone?

And his body hair?

"Oh god no!" Chelle screamed.

Blake whipped around, spitting out bits of supercheese mustache, ready to do his best ninja moves on whatever threatened his sugarplum.

And stopped when he saw her horrified face as she cradled a pair of massive breasts, unencumbered by anything like a bra.

Before Blake could work out any sort of intelligible words, someone in a window above their heads yelled something in a language he'd never heard.

From the nearby buildings poured throng after horde of cheering, clapping people. Men, mostly, plus a few women. Although it wasn't easy to tell which except for the bearded ones.

All of them wore similar long shapeless robes in yellows, reds, and oranges. Blake felt like they were being rushed by all the leaves he'd ever blown into a neighbor's yard.

"Welcome to Autregia," Dunkel yelled over the general ruckus. "A lovely little dimension which truly appreciates your art form, Mr. Thompson. Ms. Parker."

Blake couldn't make heads or tails of the crowd's gabble, but the drooling leers and ridiculous hip thrusts made it clear what art form they appreciated.

"I apologize for the rather chilly welcome," Dunkel went on. "I took the liberty of adjusting your physical forms back to their former splendor. And those slacks and golf shirts simply wouldn't do, I'm afraid."

"I am *not* dealing with these horrible things again," Chelle said, tears streaming down her face. "My back already hurts!"

Dunkel waggled a finger that desperately needed breaking off.

"Tut, tut. A few dozen live performances, and you'll be able to redesign yourself however you like."

Blake snuck a glance back the way they'd come. Saw the gloriously uncomplicated office through a perfectly round hole in the air.

"Let's not be too hasty, Chelle," he said, taking her hand and giving it a quick double squeeze. *Trust me,* that double squeeze said. "Let's hear the man out."

Still holding her hand, Blake turned to Dunkel. "How about introducing us to your friends, Mr. Dunkel? And if you dig their jive, help us translate terms and conditions."

Dunkel clapped his hands like a little kid.

"I simply knew you'd see reason, Mr. Thompson!"

He stepped around Blake and Chelle, raising his hands over his head and shouting something in hip-thruster.

"Go!" Blake yelled, sweeping his bare leg forward, catching Dunkel right at the ankles and sending him crashing to the ground. Not a bad ninja move at all.

Chelle didn't need telling twice. As soon as Blake moved, she ran back through the hole thingie, Blake hot on her heels.

And just like that, their clothes were back and Chelle could stand up straight without straining. The fur on Blake's lip was gone too, thank whoever might be listening upstairs.

Through the whatever-it-was, he saw Dunkel getting back to his feet. He was yelling and waving at the kaftan-clad crowd, but none of them seemed remotely interested in getting near a hole that sucked you into someplace not at all like home.

One thing about knowing how to fix something was Blake and Chelle also knew how to *un*-fix it.

He yanked on the giant blade switch, shoving it back up to its original position.

The rainbow swirls came back, blocking out the adobe buildings and berobed pervsters before fading away.

Blake took the rare earth magnet he always kept in his tool bag and dropped it in the middle of the contraption's drive array.

Chelle jerked the copper cable loose and used it to whip the vacuum tubes into sparkly dust.

Panting from the exertion, they ran back up the long hallway and through the mirrored door into a blast of swampy air.

Blake had never been so happy to sweat in his life.

They jumped in the van and laid black streaks all the way back to the road.

"Want to talk about it?" Chelle asked as she slowed to a less cop-attracting speed.

"Nope."

Blake leaned his head back and rubbed his upper lip. No dead lemur, thank goodness.

"Sugarplum?"

"Yeah, sweetie?"

Blake took her hand again, lacing his fingers through hers.

"How about we stick with skinflint accountants from now on?"

JASON A. ADAMS

Author of *GS-304* and *Sunlit Dispositions*

SPECIAL DELIVERY

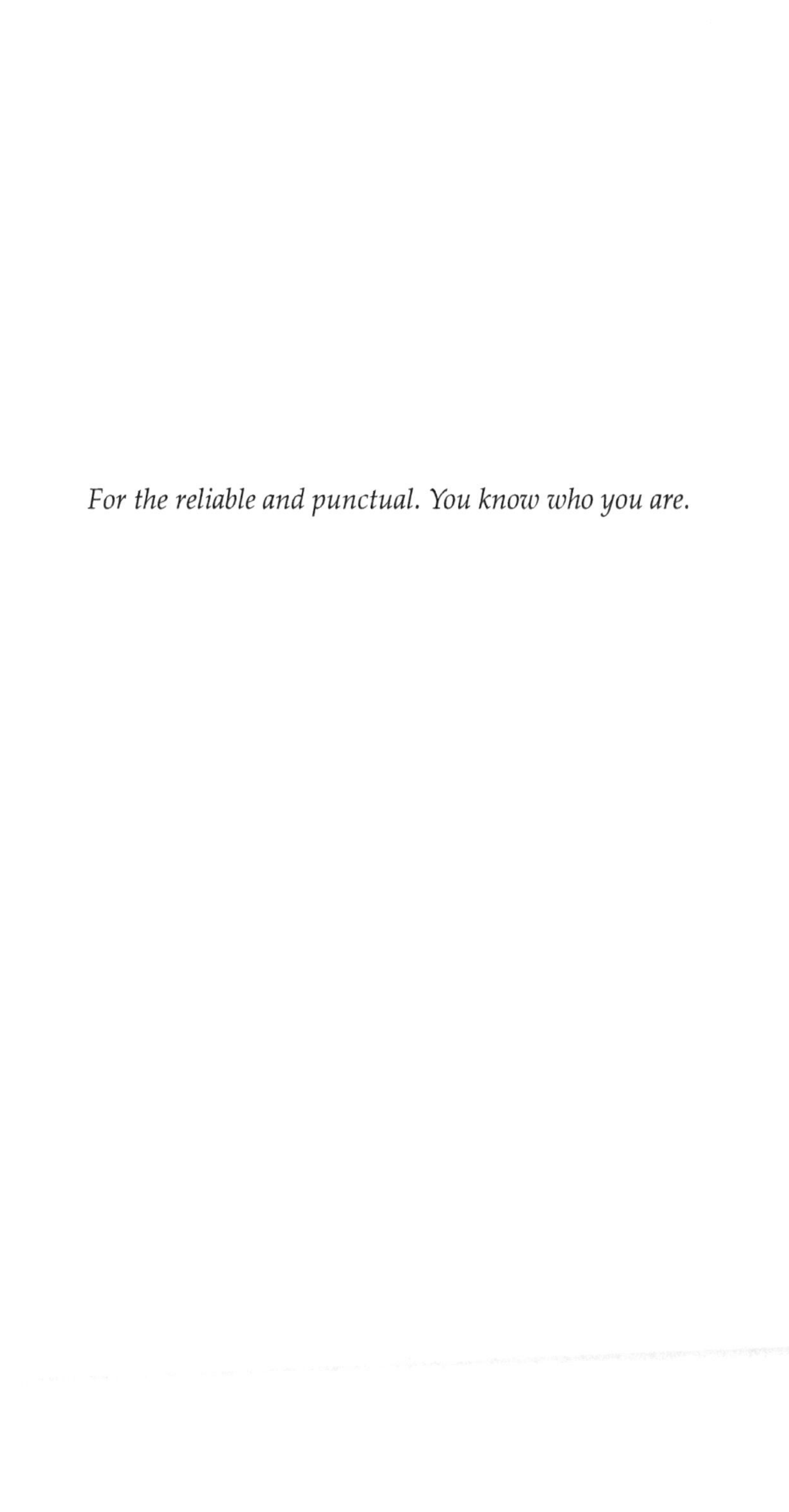

For the reliable and punctual. You know who you are.

Chapter 1

The mail is usually extremely reliable.

Not that Ted Jenkins thought much about the reliability of the mail. At least not until the letter showed up.

His day had started out the way it always did. Just the way he liked it.

Alarm at 6:45 in the morning. Lay the covers over and get out of bed while the gentle yellow glow of the sunrise lamp slowly lights the sensible eggshell-white walls of his bedroom.

Floss, brush, minty mouthwash, potty break. Then a ten-minute shower with his usual shampoo and body wash that filled the room with the steamy scent of indeterminate citrus and condensed against the easy-to-clean white tiles.

Today's towel and washcloth in the hamper, tomorrow's pulled from the stack of identical items in the simple chrome hutch behind the commode, to be draped over the shower rod, ready to go for the next day's ablutions.

Both towels and washcloths kept as white as untouched snow by his own blend of borax and bleach. If any picked up a recalcitrant stain, in the garbage it went. He had a contact at a local hotel supply outlet, and could get all the reliable white linens he needed.

With the daily body maintenance handled, he gave a quick run of the comb through hair kept at precisely half-an-inch long (trimmed at Jasper's barber shop on the second Saturday of every month), and donned white jockeys along with today's black cargo pants and green polo shirt, taken from the left side of a closet rod lined with neatly creased duplicates. In the evening, shirt and trousers would join the towel and washcloth in the hamper, and be returned to the right side of the closet after their Sunday afternoon laundering.

In the kitchen, Ted popped a medium-roast coffee pod into the stainless-steel single-cup brewer sitting on the pearly solid-surface countertop. In the one minute it took to brew, he took a boiled egg from the refrigerator, peeled and mashed it onto one half of an English muffin. Consuming breakfast and coffee consumed another two minutes. Another minute to rinse and rack his coffee cup, and to wipe the counter and sweep the pristine white linoleum floor for any stray crumbs.

Ready to face another day tuning and monitoring the database servers he loved, Ted collected his black laptop bag from its spot beside the door, checked his pockets for keys and wallet, and...

And stopped just before his hand found the doorknob.

On the tan mat below the mail slot lay a cream-colored #10 envelope. Nine-and-a-half inches by just over four. Standard business size.

Ted jumped when his watch buzzed, letting him

know the #46 bus was due in five minutes. He should be halfway down the sidewalk toward Walker Street by now, but the envelope had thrown him.

Two forty-five in the afternoon. That was when the mail carrier pushed everything through the slot, according to his doorbell-slash-security camera. Two forty-five, give or take a maddening three to ten minutes. Not sometime in the wee hours of the morning.

The envelope didn't seem threatening. He could see his name and address printed in non-threatening and reliable Times New Roman. Fourteen point, which was a bit unnecessary, but he'd seen it before. A logo in the upper left corner he hadn't seen before, but couldn't quite make out from where he stood.

His watch buzzed again. Two minutes to get to the corner of Walker and 13th to catch his bus.

The envelope would have to wait. He didn't go through his mail until he got home at 6:30, barring any traffic or construction on the bus route.

Carefully stepping over the offending rectangle of paper on the foyer floor, Ted opened the white six-paneled door and continued his reliable routine.

But he could feel the envelope sitting on his mat. Exactly like it shouldn't be.

Not before two forty-five, plus or minus.

Chapter 2

The whole day felt off.

Ted made it to work by eight forty-seven as usual, although he'd had to walk rapidly to catch his bus.

At the office, everything went as it should. His servers churned away, crunching data as reliably as ever. The same annoying coworkers made the same annoying jokes about his punctuality and lack of wardrobe flexibility, which he ignored.

Ted stuck to his well-organized cubicle. System checks took up two hours and twenty minutes of his morning.

Two hours and twenty-*eight* minutes.

Ted had to go over the numbers a couple of times to be sure they were accurate, his concentration less reliable than it usually was.

What was in that envelope?

Maybe it was a bill? But no, that couldn't be it. He had reminders set in both his work calendar and on the paper calendar over the coffee machine at home. Each due date marked in red, or with a sharp *ping* sound for the digital version.

He didn't take lunch until ten minutes past noon, which meant he'd have to adjust his schedule for the rest of the day. *And* the vending machine was out of tuna salad sandwiches. He had to eat pimiento cheese instead, which he could taste all the way through the three o'clock reports.

Maybe it was a charity solicitation. Some do-gooder organization delivered it by hand to save on postage. But hadn't he seen a red meter stamp? That implied an electronic postage meter, which probably meant a regular business.

Ted jumped again when his watch buzzed at five, reminding him to collect his things and head for the bus stop.

He checked his laptop screen, saw that he'd yet to submit his final daily reports and update his time sheet.

Acid roiled in his gut as he quickly finished up for the day, sweating over not having time to go through everything a couple more times before shutting down.

He made it to the bus stop at five-sixteen, giving him plenty of time to try and relax before his ride home. Which turned out to be a disturbing challenge.

All day long, he'd been off his game. Ted liked to think of himself as one of the company's most reliable employ-ees. He certainly did everything in his power to make sure his database servers operated at peak reliability.

But today he'd been distracted. Scattered.

All because of a stupid envelope on his doormat.

Several hours before *any* mail had a right to invade his doormat.

Chapter 3

TED OPENED his door at six-thirty sharp. At least the bus was reliable.

A small scatter of envelopes and grocery store circulars hid *the* envelope, at least until he scooped up the whole mess.

Dropping his laptop bag in the hall—where it promptly fell over and spilled notepad and pens across the doormat—Ted took the pile of mail to the kitchen table.

Political donation requests. *Database Admins of America* newsletter. His mother's weekly card.

And *the* envelope.

Now that it was in his hand, Ted could make out the logo in the upper left corner. A green circle sprouted green inky wings around interlocked capital letters, *C.U.M.* Below these, in tiny italics (eight point?), what looked like a slogan.

"Let Our Frazzbol Fill Your Life's Bowl"

What nonsense.

Ted looked for his letter opener. Didn't see it. Must've left it on his computer desk in the other room.

Slitting open the envelope with a butter knife (and feeling a bit like a rebel for doing so), Ted snorted. Had to be a joke. Frazzbol? Life's bowl?

He took a sheet of tri-folded lightweight printer paper from the envelope, wondering who was pranking him this time. Maybe Murray from end-user support. No discipline down in EUS. Those folks always—

Had to be a joke.

Ted scanned the letter a second time, but nothing changed with an extra read-through.

Dear Mr. Jenkins:

We hope you are enjoying your Frazzbol 3000, our newest and most powerful Frazzbol. While we believe all functions are self-evident, should you need any assistance please do not hesitate to contact us.

We do wish to remind you that your first payment of CK^2,437 (two thousand, four-hundred, thirty-seven Canusamex Krond) is one week past due. We understand that the joy of owning your own Frazzbol may have held all your attention, but we respectfully request that you remit your payment in full by the end of next week, to avoid any collection attempts.

Again, we wish you and your Frazzbol nothing but excitement and happiness!

. . .

Sincerely,
 Augustine J. Cromlech
 Canusamex Heavy Industries
 Quadrant Delta, Mexzone 37-F

Okay, this *had* to be Murray. Ted didn't know anyone else with that much of a comic-book brain. Not anyone else who had access to his home address, anyway.

He crumpled the offending piece of paper and tossed it, along with its envelope, in the trash.

Let's see. Thursday night. Pizza night.

Ted put the whole nasty business out of his mind as he dialed Johnny's Pizza and started ordering, only to be cut off by the young woman on the other end of the line.

"Don't worry, Mr. Jenkins," she said. "I recognize your number. One large thin, extra cheese and olive, right?"

He agreed happily, feeling the tension drain away as they finalized the transaction.

Good ol' Johnny's. Most reliable pies in the city.

Chapter 4

THE NEXT WEEK passed like clockwork, just the way Ted liked it.

Construction on the midtown connector was finished, so the buses all ran right on time. The HR database server he'd been tweaking now ran at 99.4% efficiency, which wasn't too shabby if he did say so himself.

Best of all, the only mail he got all week wasn't on the mat until he got home in the evenings. And none of it had bogus logos or return addresses.

At least not until Thursday.

Ted sat on his turf-green sofa, part of a matching living room suite from the hotel supply place and perfectly plain and easy to clean. He was leafing through the latest brochures from one of the database vendors (like they needed an upgrade; the current system was plenty reliable, and he knew the software backwards and forwards) when someone knocked on his front door.

Ted checked his watch. Johnny's Pizza was reliable

to a T, but he'd only called in his order ten minutes ago.

Grumbling and grousing, he marked his place in the brochure and went to answer the door.

Which might have been his biggest mistake of the year.

Standing on the front stoop stood a strangely skinny dark-haired man in an oddly-cut three-piece suit.

Ted thought it was a suit, anyway. But jacket, pants, and vesty-sort-of-thing shimmered and flashed in blues and violets, like technicolor tinfoil.

"Mr. Jenkins?" the man said, checking a small transparent square held in his left hand. "I'm Augustine Cromlech, Collection Officer number Three-Seven-Seven, Camusamex Industries. I believe you received a communication from my office recently. May I come in?"

Last week's letter flashed through Ted's brain as he tried to find some reliable words to put together.

"I think there's been a mistake," he managed. "I didn't order anything from you people."

Cromlech tapped the pad.

"I believe you'll find you certainly did," he said. "One Frazzbol 3000, series J, in chartreuse camel hair. Delivered COD, yet my company has not received the C."

Ted's palm was slick against the door, and his ordinarily reliable anti-perspirant was letting him down.

"Look, Mr…ah…Cromlech. I don't even know what a frazzbol is or why I'd want one. I certainly didn't order anything from any Canusamex Industries."

Cromlech raised his rather-tufty eyebrows.

"What a Frazzbol *is?* Come now, Mr. Jenkins. Easier

to ask what it isn't. Why, a Frazzbol is the perfect companion, compatriot, and comrade anyone could ask for! By the way, have you asked your Frazzbol what it can do for you? I think you'll find—"

"I don't *have* a Frazzbol!" Ted erupted. "I don't *want* a Frazzbol! Come inside and check for yourself, since you're the only one here that would *recognize* a Frazzbol!"

Cromlech started to say something, but stopped. He peered over Ted's shoulder. Scanned the room behind. First with his eyes, then waving the plastic square in his left hand. Which bleeped and flashed orange a couple of times.

"Hm. I see."

Good thing, because Ted didn't.

"Mr. Jenkins," Cromlech said, looking at his tablet again. "Mr. Theodosic Jenkins, 373 Plainview Lane, Quadrant Epsilon, USA Zone 15-A?"

"Theo-who?" Ted asked. "It's Theodore. Ted. And this is Akron. Ohio. Not whatever quadrant or zone."

Cromlech scowled down at his pad. Waved it around some more until it bleeped again. Read whatever it had to say.

"When I get my hands on those clowns in dispatch…"

Finally he looked back at Ted and held out his twinkly-cuffed hand.

"My apologies, Mr. Jenkins. I see there's been a mixup in our accounts department. Please do not think we run our business like this all the time."

"It's okay," Ted said, shaking Cromlech's cool hand. "Mixups happen. Reliability always needs improving."

"Thank you for your understanding." He took a card from an inner pocket of his jacket and held it out.

Ted accepted it, saw the same winged green circle logo over Cromlech's name.

"If you have any other questions or concerns, please don't hesitate to contact me. Simply press your thumb against the circle, and I'll be in touch as soon as I'm free."

Ted nodded. Stuck the card in his pants pocket.

"Like I said, these things happen. Best of luck tracking down the other Jenkins."

Cromlech gave the sort of thin-lipped, sour-lemon smile that only came with having to sort out someone else's mess. He bowed, then spun around and headed for the sidewalk.

Ted didn't watch him go. He shut the door. Took the card from his pocket. Tore it into the smallest pieces he could and shoved it all the way to the bottom of the trashcan.

When the doorbell rang again about twelve minutes later, Ted had almost managed to forget the whole sorry business. That should be the delivery driver from Johnny's with Ted's cheese and olive pizza.

But it wasn't.

When Ted opened the door, his view was blocked by a heavy crate that looked like plastic or PVC or something.

The huge white box, unmarked except for a depressingly familiar green wing-and-circle logo, reached almost all the way to the porch light, and was just as wide on both sides.

A plastic holder adhered to the front held what looked like a packing slip.

With shaking hands, Ted tore the holder open and removed the slip.

Unfolding the slip as a car with a lit-up *Johnny's*

sign on the roof came to a stop at the curb, Ted saw that his fears were completely justified.

Mr. Jenkins. We hope you will enjoy your new Frazzbol 3000! Please don't hesitate to ask your Frazzbol 3000 for installation and feeding instructions.

In front of him, the giant crate suddenly rocked as something inside shifted.

Ted wondered how hard it would be to tape Cromlech's card back together.

JASON A. ADAMS

Author of *GS-304* and *Sunlit Dispositions*

Resurrecting Ruby

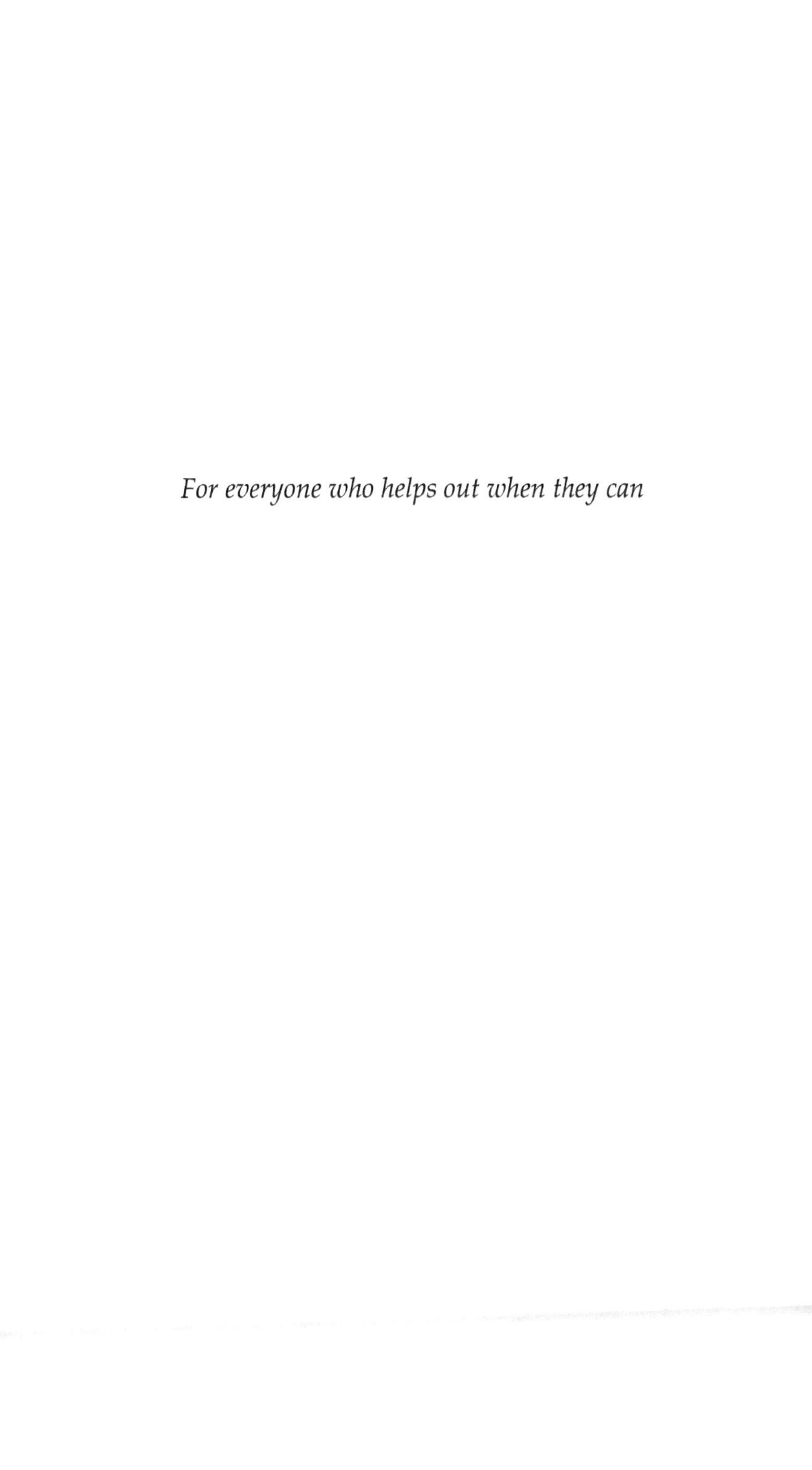

For everyone who helps out when they can

Chapter 1

The first of March means new beginnings.

Snow still hides in the shady places. But here and there, bright crocuses poke their white, violet, or yellow heads up through the half-frozen soil, making yards and meadows look like Easter egg hunting grounds.

Rising temperatures free the scents of loam, last year's leaves slowly returning to the earth. One can almost hear the sap rushing up into the sugar trees, as yet untapped and burgeoning with promise.

The oaks and sycamores still wave naked branches through the air, but Nature sweeps her green paintbrush over the maples and poplars, turning the hillsides into mint-dusted promises of warmer days on the horizon.

As the vernal equinox approaches, the morning skies fill with birdsong. Few kits or chicks grace the landscape yet, but soon the forest floor will be filled with the sound of juvenile scampering.

Spring's threshold has not yet been crossed, but a keen eye can spot it not too far away.

~

Jesse Holbrook dropped the handles of his wheelbarrow, letting the skids bounce off the gravels. He leaned back as far as he could, hands in the small of his back and pushing until he felt the snap-crackle-pop all the way up and down his poor ol' tired spine.

Afternoon sun lit the place up like a fairy land, kicking off all the dust and drops in the air, surrounding him with a zillion fireflies. Temp was just right, too. Warming his face and arms at the same time the still-chilly breeze cooled him right back down. He had his flannel draped over the fender of his truck nearby, but on days like this long sleeves were maybe-so-maybe-no.

The snow and ice had finally melted off most of the place, and that meant cleaning up winter's deadfall. Mostly sticks and branches this year, thank goodness. Not like after the big'un of ought-nine, the one that had dumped three feet of wetpack overnight and brought down most all the weaker pines. He'd worried about the huge red oak that had been anchoring the yard since before George Washington had his squabble with the redcoats.

The oak was a monster of a tree, nearly four foot thick at the base and so tall the chickadees and squirrels needed air hoses up top. Solid as the mountain she grew from, save for a wee knothole right at the base of the trunk, and that surely was no bother to such a giant.

Even after so many years and so many snows, the

hoary old elder still stood guard over the Holbrook family land, and Jesse surely was glad for that.

No, he'd not be spending near on a week trying to chainsaw his way down the driveway this year. Maybe there was a god, and maybe he was an all right ol' boy. Sometimes, anyway.

Still yet, twigs and twiddles can still wear a man out, especially one without any handy teenagers to extort for allowance money.

With a huge inhale that had his jeans button cutting deep, Jesse sucked in a lungful of Appalachian air all the way down to his toes. Couldn't call it *fresh* air, not with all the mulched leaves and wood, the rot of last year, and a whiff of some critter's dinner leftovers off in the brush, but it was a good smell for all that. Full of life and home and comfort.

Spring on the way sure did stink the mountains up right pretty.

But lordy mercy, he was tired. Maybe he'd let the rest of his yard cleaning wait a bit. No hurry, and that's just how he liked things.

He pulled a crumpled plastic bottle from his back pocket and drank a great big swallow of Tang, his favorite since he'd been knee-high to a grasshopper. Astronauts drank it, so that had to mean something. Besides, nothing beat that kinda-orange tartness after a good round of hard work.

Away off to the east, a puffy swell of dirty gray perched all along Wallens Ridge. The clouds hadn't yet spilled over the caprock. They just sat there all pert and sassy, biding their time.

Jesse checked his personal weather station. Right knee a little twingey, but not so bad he felt any snow.

Left bunion had a throb or two, but not so big he felt it without thinking on it.

Might be some rain on the way, but no snow or ice. The weather cutie on channel five had said something about a "negligible chance of precipitation," but Jesse trusted his bones more than some talking head, no matter how many syllables she put in her words.

He'd no sooner taken the weather cutie's hand for the dance hall in his imagination when those sassy clouds stopped being pert and got down to serious business, cresting up and over Wallens Ridge, spilling down the near side. They'd come in low and fast, probably skim the treetops on his own slice of mountain.

Wind was coming on, too. Leaves both damp and dry started up a reel across his yard, swirling up into mini-tornadoes when they blew around the corner of the porch.

Dang it. He'd be cleaning the yard all over again tomorrow.

Jesse took up the wheelbarrow's handles, letting go for a moment to snatch his flannel out of the air as it flapped by his head.

Time to check the genny, make sure it was good and gassed up. Wind like that and some tree or other was sure to swoon over a power line.

By the time he got the wheelbarrow back in the shed, checked his generator, and made it through the front door, he'd not have been surprised to see an old lady pedaling her bicycle past Dorothy's house.

Leaves and branches and some of the biggest raindrops he'd ever seen blew sideways past his kitchen window, while the wind squalled up a ruckus, shaking walls and windows and probably bedrock like a granny flappin' dust from her favorite quilt.

The big red oak's limbs, some bigger than most of the other trees hereabouts, waved about but nothing fell bigger than his thumb.

Well, wasn't anything he could do about a storm, except make sure fridge and freezer stayed cold. And climb up after to hammer down the nails in the roof tin that were sure to wriggle loose with all the help from the gale.

The kitchen light flickered a couple of times as he lit the gas on his trusty Kenmore range and started a pot of soup beans. He'd let the pintos simmer until bedtime, then sit and cool all night. Be just right for lunch tomorrow, and he'd probably need an extra helping with the way the runoff from the hill behind the house had started cutting through the driveway gravels.

His back already ached at the thought of the mattock, rake, and shovel in his near future.

Well, hell. Time for a bowl of tomato soup and a fried baloney on sourdough. He'd check in on channel five, see if Ms. Weather Cutie had anything to say about the "negligible chance of precipitation" currently carrying his driveway off to rebuild Louisiana.

Chapter 2

AN EARTH-SHATTERING crash jolted Jesse awake just as the Final Jeopardy jingle wrapped up.

"What is Van Diemen's Land," he muttered at the gray-haired Canadian on the tube, not bothering to wait for confirmation. Except for a squeal of victory from one of the contestants, everything was quiet. Oh, the old house creaked and groaned a little, relaxing back into its bed after having its feathers ruffled, but the wind had died and he heard no *plink* of rain hitting the tin roof.

Yawning so big his jaws popped, he shuffled to the kitchen window and looked out to check the damage.

And gave his own house-worthy groan.

The yard outside was invisible under a couple of tons of jagged, splintered red oak limbs.

He couldn't see the leviathan's trunk through the mess, but neither could he see the old tree standing tall and proud anymore.

Overhead, the clouds had gone on their way,

leaving a few of the most perky stars to shine through the light of a full moon bigger'n a jumbo Moon Pie. The silvery light lit everything up like the spot on a woman singing slow jazz. More than bright enough to see the remains of the giant red oak stretched out on the muddy ground.

Jesse had to blink a mile a minute as he pulled on his rubber mud boots. It was only a tree. No big deal. Plenty of other trees on the mountain.

But none of them so big or old or stately as *his* tree.

He stumped across the porch, down the steps, and toward where the tree had stood until a few minutes ago.

Terrible as he felt about the oak's death, Jesse couldn't help but be awed at the exposed root ball, now vertical instead of horizontal and at least twice and a half as tall as he was.

By some miracle from a good ol' boy upstairs, his truck was untouched save for a few splashes of mud.

Shed? Fine.

House? Sturdy and whole as ever.

Driveway? Well, looked like he'd be chainsawing his way out after all.

Sniffling a self-pitying sniffle, Jesse headed back inside. He'd start on the cleanup tomorrow, once he had some daylight.

He dreamed of the old guardian oak all night long. Dreams that took him back to when he'd been just a little feller.

Of playing all around the base.

Of his papaw fetching his tallest ladder up against the trunk so Jesse could climb up into the branches and be a right little Tarzan.

Of days spent leaned up against the old girl, reading books about fairies and witches and magic and…

Chapter 3

JESSE WOKE to sunbeams filling his little bedroom. Except where long, gnarled shadows blocked the light. Shadows cast by the stiff arms of a dead thing.

He sighed, dreading the work ahead. Still, he got up, got his work clothes on, and went to fetch saw and wheelbarrow so he could start breaking the old girl down as best he could.

It took Jesse a fair bit to get everything together. His saw oil had snuck off and how in the world had it ended up on the floor under his bench grinder? Blade was dull, so he'd spent a quarter of an hour filing the teeth sharp again.

By the time he finally made it back to the yard, the sun stood proud right overhead. The air was full of the pitter and patter of mud falling from the upper roots on the upended ball as it slowly dried out, along with the oak's veins.

The big storm from yesterday had blown itself along down the ridges, but a breeze ruffled Jesse's hair and sent a few leaves skittering across what little yard wasn't buried under the tree.

Funny how a low sound like that can sound just like…

"Hey, now! Watch yourself, big fella!"

Jesse jumped so bad he near tossed the wheelbarrow clean down the mountain.

"Yeah! Mind your feet and manners, big'un!"

Sounded like two different folks, but tiny. Like those old Disney cartoons with the oversized rat and his buddies.

Then a whole babble of those squeaky complainers started up, all from down around Jesse's kneecaps.

"Some of use are tryin' to work, Bubba!"

"Didn't your mamma teach you no manners?"

"If you can't lend a hand, at least lend your backside and scoot!"

Jesse figured he'd bonked his head on one of the roots or branches sticking out every whichaway. He looked down, and saw a milling crowd of itty-bitty little men, and a few teeny little women, judging from the swells in the bibs of their overalls.

All of them looked of a type. That is, a type that looked just like Jesse's granddad and great-granddaddy had looked.

All wore patched and stitched faded denim biballs and heavy brown muck boots. The ones with the puffy chests wore long-sleeve shirts in washed-too-much gray. The flat-chested ones showed hairy little chests and arms.

They were all pretty hairy all over. Mustaches and beards covered every face, except where their beady little eyes peeked out beneath eyebrows so long and bushy you could strain soup through them. Even their ears were hairy, just as hairy as his papaw's had been.

But Papaw's ears hadn't been near so pointy.

"'Scuse me," Jesse said. If he'd knocked himself silly, might as well run with it. "I surely didn't mean to get in y'all's way."

The gabble-babble started up all over again, until one old-timer (Jesse thought. Hard to tell since gray was only one of a dozen different hair colors, most of which belonged in a Crayola box) shushed the others with a gesture and a couple of good-natured brain-dusters to the backs of heads.

"That's fine, young feller," he said. "Looks to me like you might be on the same errand as us. You caught ary notion on how to stand Ruby back on her feet?"

Jesse scratched his head and looked around. He didn't see anyone laying down on the job.

"Ruby's what we call yon oak maiden, son," the boss said with that slow patience that means somebody's checked their good sense at the door. "Who else looks like they need helpin'? Besides, she's most of our roof, you know."

The little guy stuck out a little hand. "Name's Patchweed Duckfoot," he said. "You can call me Patch. You'd be Jesse, right? I recollect your pap tellin' me about your mamma whelpin' you a little ways back."

"Pleased to meet you, Patch," Jesse said, shaking the tiny hand as best he could. A little ways back? He'd never see fifty again, and his pap had passed right after Jesse blew out three candles on his cake.

"As to your question, I can't say I'd given it any thought." Jesse took a long look at the remains of his guardian oak. Ruby, according to Patch. Who might or might not be a concussed brain shorting itself out. "I don't have a crane big enough to hoist her back up, and I doubt my back's up to me laying hold."

Jesse chuckled.

Patch didn't.

No, the little guy scratched under his whiskers as he squinted first at the exposed roots, then back up at Jesse.

"You've lived here your whole life, ain't that so?"

"Most of it, sure," Jesse said. "I was away for a bit with the Army, but that didn't take and back I came when my first time was up."

"How well do you know Ruby?"

Jesse must've had the stupid-eye again, because Patch gave out another big sigh.

"The tree, boy. The tree. How well do you know her?"

Patch lifted up the cuff at Jesse's right ankle and poked his bare shin. Hard. And kept right on digging his knobbly little finger in deep. Probably would leave a brui…

The yard, the dead oak tree, the crowd of little folk all faded away as images exploded across the insides of Jesse's eyeballs.

Again he played around the big guardian tree.

Climbed up its branches.

Read himself into a doze up against her trunk.

Collected acorns so he could make a squirrel feeder.

Watched as the leaves went from mint-colored buds to deep emerald leaves to scarlet brighter than a working girl's lipstick to brown snowflakes drifting down at Fall's end.

The world snapped back into place when Patch pulled his finger out of the dent in Jesse's shin meat.

"Not bad at all, big'un. We know Ruby's backside

better'n our own. 'Twixt us and you, we orta be able to do a thing or two." He cupped his hands around his whiskers and gave a whistle that had Jesse worried about his windows.

"Y'all get your worthless hides up top so we can do this thing!"

For such a wee set of lungs, Patch's shout lit up the mountain, bouncing back and forth between the ridges until Jesse's ears rang like the Hunchback's bell.

Up from the hole where Ruby the Red Oak used to sit, up a spiraling set of tiny little stairs that led right to where the knothole at the base of her trunk used to be, trooped an army of knee-high, biball-wearing, whisker-sprouting little folk. Both of the prominent chest variety and not.

"Now you just think on Ruby here, as many of those same pictures as you can recollect," Patch said, as the miniature regiment linked their hands in a ring that spread all the way around the fallen oak tree.

Jesse tried, but it was hard to look at what was left of his family's guardian tree. Damn shame to see her laid out like that, instead of reaching her fingers up toward the sun. Sad to see a broken bird's nest, that by rights should be up where the birdies inside could touch the sky.

Jesse smiled, recalling a passel of spring chicks twittering away over the years. The squirrel kits that chased each other through the canopy, spending their playing years in the same tree they'd bear their own young in the next spring. That progression of colors from one season to the next. Watching the old girl dress up and then down as spring passed through summer to fall and then to winter's sleep.

In their ring around the tree, dozens of wee voices

raised up in a low, thrumming hum, not at all like the fifesong they'd spoken before.

The hairs all up down Jesse's body stood to attention, like he'd wool-socked across the world's biggest carpet.

A glow filled his vision. A glow first pale and minty, then as green as fresh money, then as red as a classic candy-apple muscle car.

The humming got louder. Jesse found himself humming along, the words of a song from one of the fairy tales he'd read under this very tree running through his mind.

His very bones vibrated with the sound of all those voices. His eyeballs jittered in their sockets as the green-red-brown lights drowned out the sun, but not before he saw Ruby standing tall and proud, not laying on the ground a dead thing.

He'd have sworn he saw her stretch and arch just like he did when his back fussed about hard work.

Every voice on the mountain from critters with any number of legs raised up in a shout that threatened to split the bones of the earth.

Jesse could *taste* that shout, just like he could *see* Ruby's rough bark, and *hear* the green growing scent of her summer leaf-dress.

The shout shut off like a switch had been thrown.

The glow faded down to nothing, but nothing replaced in Jesse's vision.

He swayed once. Twice.

Then followed his shadow until he landed right on top of it.

Chapter 4

A LEAF BLOWING across Jesse's nose sneezed him awake.

Usually, he had to work at finding a real wakeup, but not this time. Everything he'd seen and heard slammed back into his brain like a truck.

He jumped up to his feet, not the least bit sore even after a nap on the dirt.

There sat his wheelbarrow, still loaded with chainsaw, gas, and other tools.

And there stood the Holbrook guardian oak.

Ruby.

No branches scattered over the ground at all.

The yard around her thick trunk was mossy and smooth, save where her roots humped the ground.

Like nothing had ever happened.

Probably *hadn't* happened. Jesse snorted. Rubbed the back of his neck.

Couldn't have happened. He'd tripped. Bumped his noggin a good one.

That was it.

But why would he have the chainsaw out? Maybe

he knocked himself silly, but not out? He'd been walking around in a haze, living out his dream?

Jesse took in the whole of the yard.

Must've done better with the cleanup yesterday than he thought. He didn't see any twigs or branches still to gather up.

And all the ruts the rain had dug through the gravels were gone. The driveway was just as smooth as…

Jesse scratched his head again.

And laughed out loud. Laughed like a little boy who still believed in wonders.

He walked around Ruby's trunk until he spotted the knothole at the base, the gray scarring around the smoother wood inside looking just like a…

Jesse hunkered down on his knees. Raised his knuckles.

And knocked.

ABOUT JASON

Jason A. Adams writes across the spectrum. His stories include science fiction, fantasy, horror, Appalachian folk tales, and sometimes a little romance here and there.

You can find more of his work and sign up for updates from his Brain Squirrels at www.jason-adams.info, and in the pages of *Pulphouse Magazine*, most recently in issue #10. His stories have also appeared in the 2019 and 2020 Winter Holiday Spectaculars from WMG Publishing. Several more stories will appear in upcoming issues of *Pulphouse Magazine* and Holiday Spectaculars, so stay tuned!

Jason, a recovering Air Force brat who grew up all over the US and Japan, now perches in the mountains of Southwest Virginia with his beautiful wife Kari Kilgore, four spoiled cats, and assorted wild visitors from the nearby forest.

news@jasonadams.info

facebook.com/Jason.A.Adams.2

ALSO BY JASON A. ADAMS

I hope you enjoyed reading the stories in *Through the Squirrel Tree* as much as I enjoyed writing them.

Visit www.jasonadams.info and join the adventure for exclusive new fiction, my past and future travels, and whatever else strikes my fancy. Hope to see you there!

Novellas:

Agonist

Short Stories:

Mick of Malvern: Seeker for Hire (A Hard-Boiled Fairy Tale)

To Catch a Thief (An Appalachian Gothic Tale)

Sunlit Dispositions (A Hard-Boiled Space Opera)

GS-304

Angel of Mercy

Cupids

The Green Knight

Oppositional

Birth of the Makmorn

Collections and Anthologies:

Near Future Forward (with Kari Kilgore)

Partners in Romance (with Kari Kilgore)

Tales From the Squirrel Garden: Volume 1

ADDITIONAL COPYRIGHT INFORMATION